What Kids Say About
Carole Marsh Mysteries . . .

I love the real locations! Reading the book always makes me want to go and visit them all on our next family vacation. My Mom says maybe, but I can't wait!

One day, I want to be a real kid in one of Ms. Marsh's mystery books. I think it would be fun, and I think I am a real character anyway. I filled out the application and sent it in and am keeping my fingers crossed!

History was not my favorite subject till I starting reading Carole Marsh Mysteries. Ms. Marsh really brings history to life. Also, she leaves room for the scary and fun.

I think Christina is so smart and brave. She is lucky to be in the mystery books because she gets to go to a lot of places. I always wonder just how much of the book is true and what is made up. Trying to figure that out is fun!

Grant is cool and funny! He makes me laugh a lot!!

I like that there are boys and girls in the story of different ages. Some mysteries I outgrow, but I can always find a favorite character to identify with in these books.

They are scary, but not too scary. They are funny. I learn a lot. There is always food which makes me hungry. I feel like I am there.

What Parents and Teachers Say About Carole Marsh Mysteries . . .

I think kids love these books because they have such a wealth of detail. I know I learn a lot reading them! It's an engaging way to look at the history of any place or event. I always say I'm only going to read one chapter to the kids, but that never happens—it's always two or three, at least!
—Librarian

Reading the mystery and going on the field trip—Scavenger Hunt in hand—was the most fun our class ever had! It really brought the place and its history to life. They loved the real kids characters and all the humor. I loved seeing them learn that reading is an experience to enjoy!
—4th grade teacher

Carole Marsh is really on to something with these unique mysteries. They are so clever; kids want to read them all. The Teacher's Guides are chock full of activities, recipes, and additional fascinating information. My kids thought I was an expert on the subject—and with this tool, I felt like it!
—3rd grade teacher

My students loved writing their own Real Kids/Real Places mystery book! Ms. Marsh's reproducible guidelines are a real jewel. They learned about copyright and more & ended up with their own book they were so proud of!
—Reading/Writing Teacher

"The kids seem very realistic—my children seemed to relate to the characters. Also, it is educational by expanding their knowledge about the famous places in the books."

"They are what children like: mysteries and adventures with children they can relate to."

"Encourages reading for pleasure."

"This series is great. It can be used for reluctant readers, and as a history supplement."

The Counterfeit
CONSTITUTION
MYSTERY

by

Carole Marsh

Published by Gallopade International/Carole Marsh Books. Printed in the United States of
America.

Managing Editor: Sherry Moss
Senior Editor: Janice Baker
Assistant Editor: Beverly Melasi
Cover Design: Mark Mackey, Rightsyde Graphics
Picture Credits: Mike Yother, Hoodie-Hoo Studios
Content Design: M. K. Whitaker
Cover Photo Credits: Christine Balderas, ©Images from Photos.com
Cover Illustrations Credits: Miros Lav Kolar, Rebecca Lowe, Georgia Longford

Gallopade International is introducing SAT words that kids need to know in each new book
that we publish. The SAT words are bold in the story. Look for this special logo **SAT**
beside each word in the glossary. Happy Learning!

Heelys is a registered trademark of Heelys, Inc.

Gallopade is proud to be a member and supporter of these educational organizations and
associations:

American Booksellers Association
American Library Association
International Reading Association
National Association for Gifted Children
The National School Supply and Equipment Association
The National Council for the Social Studies
Museum Store Association
Association of Partners for Public Lands
Association of Booksellers for Children

20 YEARS AGO . . .

As a mother and an author, one of the fondest periods of my life was when I decided to write mystery books for children. At this time (1979) kids were pretty much glued to the TV, something parents and teachers complained about the way they do about video games today.

I decided to set each mystery in a real place—a place kids could go and visit for themselves after reading the book. And I also used real children as characters. Usually a couple of my own children served as characters, and I had no trouble recruiting kids from the book's location to also be characters.

Also, I wanted all the kids—boys and girls of all ages—to participate in solving the mystery. And, I wanted kids to learn something as they read. Something about the history of the location. And I wanted the stories to be funny.

That formula of real+scary+smart+fun served me well. The kids and I had a great time visiting each site and many of the events in the stories actually came out of our experiences there. (For example, we really did stick our toes in the cold ocean, climb Jockey's Ridge, and see Flyer for ourselves!)

I love getting letters from teachers and parents who say they read the book with their class or child, then visited the historic site and saw all the places in the mystery for themselves. What's so great about that? What's great is that you and your children have an experience that bonds you together forever. Something you shared. Something you both cared about at the time. Something that crossed all age levels—a good story, a good scare, a good laugh!

20 years later,

Carole Marsh

Hey, kids! As you see—here we are ready to embark on another of our exciting Carole Marsh Mystery adventures! You know, in "real life," I keep very close tabs on Christina, Grant, and their friends when we travel. However, in the mystery books, they always seem to slip away from Papa and I so that they can try to solve the mystery on their own!

I hope you will go to www.carolemarshmysteries.com and apply to be a character in a future mystery book! Well, the *Mystery Girl* is all tuned up and ready for "take-off!"

Gotta go... Papa says so! Wonder what I've forgotten this time?

Happy "Armchair Travel" Reading,

Mimi

Christina Yother   **Grant Yother**   **Rebekah Livingston**   **Reed Livingston**

ABOUT THE CHARACTERS

- Christina Yother, 10, from Peachtree City, Georgia
- Grant Yother, 7, from Peachtree City, Georgia, Christina's brother
- Rebekah Livingston as Alicia Hansen, Christina's pen pal from Washington, D.C.
- Reed Livingston as Mike Hansen, Alicia's brother

The many places featured in the book actually exist and are worth a visit! Perhaps you could read the book and follow the trail these kids went on during their mysterious adventure!

TITLES IN THE CAROLE MARSH MYSTERIES SERIES

#1   The Mystery of Biltmore House

#2   The Mystery on the Freedom Trail

#3   The Mystery of Blackbeard the Pirate

#4   The Mystery of the Alamo Ghost

#5   The Mystery on the California Mission Trail

#6   The Mystery of the Missing Dinosaurs

#7   The White House Christmas Mystery

#8   The Mystery on Alaska's Iditarod Trail

#9   The Mystery at Kill Devil Hills

#10   The Mystery in New York City

#11   The Mystery at Disney World

#12   The Mystery on the Underground Railroad

#13   The Mystery in the Rocky Mountains

#14   The Mystery on the Mighty Mississippi

#15   The Mystery at the Kentucky Derby

#16   The Ghost of the Grand Canyon

#17   The Mystery at Jamestown

#18   The Mystery in Chocolate Town

#19   The "Gosh Awful!" Gold Rush Mystery

#20   The Counterfeit Constitution Mystery

Books and Teacher's Guides are available at booksellers, libraries, school supply stores, museums, and many other locations!

And The Winner Is...
Mrs. Hudson's Fourth Grade Class!
Elsie Collier Elementary School
Mobile, Alabama

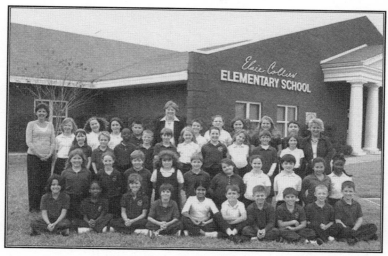

I couldn't wait to see the entries in my Carole Marsh Mysteries Classroom Contest! I was looking for just the right class with just the "right stuff" to star in my next mystery.

The winning entry captivated me right away! Mrs. Hudson's fourth grade class in Mobile, Alabama is full of fun, full of curiosity, and full of a love for social studies! They stole my heart with a letter in "pirate talk"—anyone who knows me knows how much I love pirates!

While the class in this fictional mystery is a bit rambunctious, be assured that Mrs. Hudson's class is a very well-behaved, respectful group. I am proud to feature them in my newest Real Kids, Real Places mystery!

Carole Marsh

CONTENTS

1	And The Winner Is............................	1
2	George Washington's Wild Ride.................	11
3	FBI Spy	21
4	Mini Meltdown..............................	25
5	I Spy A Spider	29
6	Blue Light Special	33
7	Let The Mystery Solving Begin.................	41
8	Colonial Constitution	45
9	Awesome Archives............................	51
10	Counterfeit Constitution?.....................	59
11	Savor The Flavor!............................	65
12	Diagram Diversion	71
13	Secret Swap	75
14	Historic Horror	79
15	Spy School	83
16	Monument Mayhem..........................	91
17	White House Wonders	99
18	You Have Bugs..............................	105
19	Top Secret	113
20	Parade of Fear	117
21	Superhero In The Sky	125
22	You're Guilty Mister	129
	About the Author............................	137
	Built-In Book Club: Talk About It!	138
	Built-In Book Club: Bring it to Life!...............	140
	Glossary	142
	Constitution Trivia...........................	143
	Be A Carole Marsh Mystery Character	145

1 AND THE WINNER IS?

"Whoooo Hoooo!"

Christina squealed with excitement.

Grant hurried into the kitchen to see what all the **commotion** was about. His sister quickly seized him around the waist.

"What are you doing?" Grant cried.

"It's here! It's here!" Christina swung him around until he thought he might throw up.

"Put me down!" he squealed between breaths.

Christina dropped him abruptly. Grant scrambled to his feet, ready to do battle with his sister, but she had already danced away towards Mimi, who was waving a red, white and blue priority mail envelope.

Rubbing his sore bottom, Grant wandered over to the counter next to his sister and grandmother. "Will anyone who's normal around here please tell me what's going on?" he asked.

Mimi let out a little breath. "A class won my contest! I can't wait to tell you who it is!" She ripped open the envelope. "And the winner is..." While Mimi slid the letter out of the envelope, Christina and Grant jockeyed for position over her shoulder.

"The Fourth Grade class from Elsie Collier Elementary School in Mobile, Alabama!" Mimi shouted. "It says here that they're going to study the U.S. Constitution soon, so we've all been invited to join them on a field trip to Washington, D.C. They've asked me to be a chaperone!"

Christina and Grant gave each other a high-five slap. "Way to go, Mimi!" shouted Grant.

Mimi slid the class picture out of the envelope. "Is that them?" Grant asked. He and Christina looked at all the smiling faces and couldn't help smiling, too. They were going to Washington, D.C.!

"Where's the phone?" Mimi asked. "I'm going to call and accept this invitation right now!" Christina listened to Mimi's side of the **conversation**. "The National Archives? Of course, that sounds wonderful. As a matter of fact, I need to go there to research my next book! What timing!"

Christina was convinced this was going to be a great adventure! Her grandmother, Mimi, who spent most of her time writing children's mystery books, loved history, and especially loved to visit Washington, D.C. To actually be in the same room with the U.S. Constitution gave Mimi goose bumps.

"Can my pen pal meet us there?" Christina asked. Christina's pen pal Alicia lived in Washington, D.C., and although they had been writing to one another for over a year, they had never met. It would be perfect timing.

"I don't see why not. I'll call Alicia's parents tonight," Mimi said.

By the next morning, everything was set. They would all leave the following weekend, and Alicia and her brother, Mike, would meet them at their hotel in Washington, D.C.

Christina heaved her yellow duffle bag atop the others waiting to be loaded into the belly of the shiny excursion bus parked at the curb of the school. As they waited for the signal to board the bus, Mimi was having second thoughts. Children were everywhere!

Some were chasing each other, while others clung desperately to their parents, as this was going to be their first trip without them. Parents were asking last-minute questions, and a woman with a megaphone was barking orders to get the children in order.

Mimi held her hands to her cheeks. "There seems to be hundreds of them!" she exclaimed to Christina.

Their teachers, Mrs. Hudson and Mrs. Whatley, heard Mimi and saw the alarm on her face. Mrs. Hudson had seen it on new chaperones before. As she approached Mimi, she laughed, stuck out her hand, and shook Mimi's with fast, friendly exuberance. "I know things seem a little crazy right now, but things will calm down," she said. "I'm Mrs. Hudson, and we are so excited to have been chosen as the winners of your contest!"

Mimi watched as one of the boys ran by and dangled a gummy worm near Christina's face.

"Stop that this instant, Thatch, or I'll call your parents and have them come and get you!" Mrs. Hudson warned. She patted her brown hair into place.

Mimi's eyes narrowed as any grandmother's would at an unruly child. She wasn't prepared for Mrs. Hudson's reply.

"Spunky little bugger," she laughed, her eyes

twinkling. She put her arm through Mimi's and led her to where the bus stood. "Come, I'll introduce you to our principal, Mrs. McRae."

They walked over to a woman with a clipboard cradled in one hand, and a megaphone in the other. She was wearing an Atlanta Braves baseball cap. Mrs. Hudson made the introductions.

"I'm delighted to meet you, Ms. Marsh. I'm a big fan of yours." Principal McRae tucked her clipboard under her arm and shook hands with Mimi. "Later, I want to ask you all about your life as a mystery writer, but for now, duty calls." She jiggled the megaphone. "It's time we get these children loaded on the bus!"

TAWEEEEEET!"

The principal put her lips to a whistle and blew into the bright blue and red megaphone. The children instantly stopped what they were doing. "Okay kids, we're going to take roll call now, just like in class," she instructed them.

"Awwww!" everyone groaned.

The megaphone returned to Mrs. McRae's

mouth. "We wouldn't want to leave anyone behind, would we?"

"Nooooooo!!"

They all shouted.

"All right then, let's load 'em up!" her voice boomed. The children hovered around her, anxiously waiting to get started.

Mrs. Hudson, standing alongside Mimi, beamed in happy anticipation. Two boys nearby were talking loudly about the fun they were going to have. "Shhhhh!" She tapped her lips. "Listen, so you hear when Mrs. McRae calls your name."

"As I call your name, please get on the bus," Mrs. McRae said. She wagged her finger at them. "One at a time, mind you."

"Delaney...Brody...Dylan...Jonathan." As Jonathan started to pass her, she stopped him. "Alright, Jonathan, give that frog to your parents. He's not going on the trip with us."

"Awwww," Jonathan said as he stepped out of line. He handed the squirming frog to his mother and ran back to the bus. His friends giggled.

"Kendle...Bradley...Jaycie...James...Kellyn...Thatch. And Thatch," she said, giving him a stern look. "I'd better not see those gummy worms in anyone's hair during the bus ride."

"Yes ma'am," he replied, his mouth full of the gooey candy. He gave the other boys a sheepish look as he boarded the bus.

"Kayla...Aiden...Katelynn...Charlie...Alyssa... Megan...Drake...Heather...Oh, and anyone who gets car sick, sit near the front, please," she advised.

On and on it went. A stream of children patiently waited their turn to board the bus as Principal McRae continued to call their names. "Tatum... Tristan... Cartasia...Madelyn...Hollie."

They boarded the bus, each jostling to be first up the steps once their name was called. When Mrs. McRae got to Emily, she paused. "All right, Emily, hand it over." The principal stuck out her hand. Emily reached into her pocket and withdrew a slingshot. "Thank you, Emily," the principal said. "You may board the bus now."

"Devon...Diamond...Kylie...Chris...Hillary... Madison." A tall, gangly boy was next in line. As Principal McRae started to call his name, she noticed that he was standing in front of her in his stocking feet. "Hold it, Gavin. Where are your shoes?" the principal asked. The other kids snickered.

Gavin hung his head. "Dylan threw them on top of the bus!" Everyone turned and looked at Dylan.

"Did not!"

"Did, too!" Gavin shot back.

"Okay, okay!" The back of Principal McRae's neck was beginning to ache, and she rubbed it with her free hand. "Let's get everyone loaded, then we'll send someone to find your shoes," she sighed.

"Joseph...Michaela...Leo...Allison...Abel...Gavin..." Mrs. McRae paused. "Oh dear, two Gavins. Well, we'll just have to watch that." She checked his name off the list. She took a deep breath and continued to call names. "Prika...Tristan...oh, another Tristan...Jeffrey, Andrew, LaFrance, and finally, Autumn," she said with a smile.

The other chaperones boarded the bus last, each shaking Mimi's hand and saying how glad they were to have her join them.

"Well, that's it," Principal McRae remarked, "except for our guest of honor, who's running a little late."

Great, I wish we could just get going, Mimi thought, as she pulled a book to read from her bag.

Suddenly, a hush came over the bus. Mimi looked up just in time to see a familiar, white-haired man trudging up the steps. George Washington had just boarded the bus!

As Mimi looked up in surprise, George Washington winked at her and took his seat across the aisle from her.

Thump! BUMP!

The bus lurched away from the curb. They were on their way to Washington, D.C.!

2 GEORGE WASHINGTON'S WILD RIDE

"Do you think Papa and Grant have left yet?" Christina asked her grandmother. Mimi glanced at her watch. "Yes, they probably have," she replied. Papa, Christina's grandfather, and Grant were meeting them at the Capital Hilton Hotel later that night. They were flying to Washington, D.C. on the *Mystery Girl*, Papa's little red and white airplane.

Once the bus lumbered onto the expressway, Mimi began to read her book about the U.S. Constitution. She pointed to a picture of our nation's leaders signing the document. "See, Christina, it says here that many of the founding fathers of the United States were at the Constitutional Convention on September 17, 1787, the night the U.S. Constitution was signed."

Curiosity got the best of Christina. "What's a founding father?" she asked.

"Our founding fathers were the political leaders who created our government and signed the Declaration of Independence and the Constitution," Mimi replied, "or who participated in the American Revolution as leaders of the patriots."

"Patriots?" Heather asked, peeking over Christina's seat back. Listening to Mimi was interesting.

"Aye, I remember it well," a deep voice remarked. George Washington stepped into the aisle near Mimi and Christina and held onto the silver rail overhead for support. "That's what we colonists called ourselves when we rebelled against British control during the American Revolution," he commented. "And our 13 colonies," he added, rubbing his chin, "became the original 13 United States."

Mrs. Hudson took her cue and stood next to the tall man wearing a white wig, a dark blue coat and tan waistcoat, and white knee breeches tucked into knee-high, black leather riding boots. A broad blue ribbon crossed over his chest.

Clap! Clap!

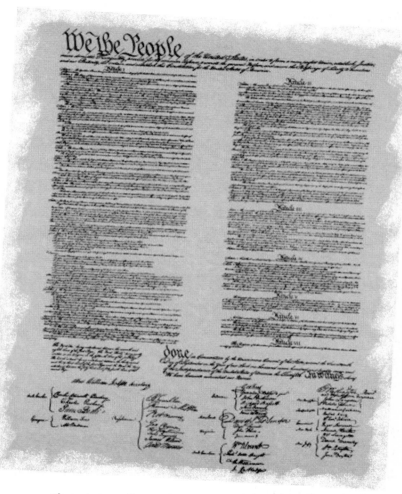

The U.S. Constitution—the foundation of U.S. government!

"Can I have your attention, please?" Mrs. Hudson asked.

After a few more snickers from the boys and SHHHHH's from the girls, the bus grew quiet.

Mrs. Hudson grabbed the edge of a seat for balance. "As you know," she explained, "there is no single person in America's history who had greater impact on the United States of America than George Washington. We are honored that General Washington could join us on our trip to talk about the U.S. Constitution." She gazed at the tall gentleman standing beside her. "General? They're all yours," she said, making a sweeping gesture with her hand.

Christina leaned forward in her seat and stole a sideways glance at Mimi. "I know he's not George Washington," she whispered, "but he sure looks like him!"

"He does look rather dashing in his uniform, doesn't he?" Mimi whispered back. "And he sounds like he knows his history. Let's help him get started."

Mimi raised her hand. "What can you tell us about the significance of the U.S. Constitution, General Washington?" she asked with genuine interest.

General Washington saw more than 50 faces staring at him, waiting for his answer. "Well," he began, "the signing of the U.S. Constitution was a giant leap in our nation's history."

"Like one giant leap for mankind like the old space program," Dylan interrupted. He looked around expectantly, hoping someone got his joke.

Alyssa rolled her eyes. "Dylan, stop trying to be funny. I'm trying to listen here," she scolded.

Mimi shifted in her seat so she could face the kids. "You know, Dylan, without the brave men early in the history of this country, the space program probably wouldn't exist," she told him.

Dylan squirmed in his seat and nodded.

"Where were we?" General Washington fiddled with the gorget, the symbol of command and status he wore around his neck. "Oh, yes. The U.S. Constitution is a living document from which we make our laws today," he said.

"It...is...aliiiiiivvve!" chanted a boy in the back. Everyone giggled.

"Class," Mrs. Hudson warned, "General Washington deserves your complete respect and attention." She narrowed her eyes at the snickering boys in the seat ahead of her. "September 17th is U.S.

Constitution Day. We WILL study the Constitution, and you WILL have to write an essay on why 39 brave men chose to sign the Constitution even though they knew it was an act of treason." The bus grew silent. "So, it's in your best interests to listen. Please continue, General," she coaxed.

"Aye." The general gave a quick tug on the lapels of his uniform and went on with his story. "Americans saw themselves as a new society, based on new principles of government. But they needed a government that would unite the states with a new set of principles to live and govern by. So, those of us in leadership," he explained, "got together with other state representatives and wrote a document so all of the 13 states would have a say in how things would be run."

"What were the new principles of government?" Hollie asked shyly.

"Basically, that the people would rule themselves, and no longer be controlled by the king of England," the general told her.

The kids were all interested by then, and Mrs. Hudson was grateful for the fun history lesson.

General Washington slowly walked down the aisle so he could give everyone a chance to ask questions. "Much of the unrest among the colonists began in the 1760s when the British government began to tighten its grip on the colonies," he explained.

"Was the king a bad man?" Gavin asked. "No one who was king and ruled a country could be bad, right?"

"No, King George III was not a bad man," General Washington answered. "England had spent a lot of money during the French and Indian War in America. He wanted to collect taxes to help pay the debt. The colonists felt they were being taxed unfairly because they had no representatives in the English government. On July 4, 1776, the Second Continental Congress issued the Declaration of Independence, telling the king that they would no longer allow him to rule them," he added, making a fist.

"What made them decide to write the U.S. Constitution?" Jaycie asked.

Mrs. Hudson saw that they were approaching their hotel. "That answer will have to wait until the next time we're all together," she replied.

"Do you really have wooden teeth?" Charlie asked.

Everyone on the bus howled with laughter.

General Washington bent down and smiled so the boy could see his gleaming white teeth. "I began to lose my teeth in my twenties," he said, "but was blessed with the finest dentures of my time made of hippopotamus ivory, gold, and a few other things," he replied.

"Cooooooolll!" the kids said, awestruck.

Mrs. Hudson thrust her arms into the air. "We've arrived!" she cried.

Everyone cheered!

3 FBI SPY

The trip had been long, and the kids were wound up from the excitement. By the time everyone got off the bus, Mimi was ready for a hot bath and a comfortable bed. She had forgotten how tough it was to keep young kids in line on a field trip! She gladly picked up the keys to her suite and tomorrow's itinerary from the hotel desk clerk.

"There's Papa and Grant!" Mimi said, waving to them. Papa looked relieved to see her. The hotel lobby was alive with giggling girls and hyperactive boys. One boy slid across the room on a tapestry rug. It stopped short of the sofa, bringing him to an abrupt halt. He fell backwards, roaring with laughter. The chaperones firmly took charge, calling names and grabbing collars to get the children to settle down and separate into their assigned groups.

Christina noticed someone jumping and waving near the front desk. "It's Alicia!" she cried, recognizing her pen pal from pictures they had e-mailed back and forth.

"Ali, how are you?" Christina said, hugging her special friend.

"I'm so glad to see you," Ali replied, "and meet your family, too! Here's my little brother, Mike."

Ali's parents had allowed Mike to come along with his sister as company for Grant. Mimi and Ali's parents had agreed that Mimi would stay in a room with Christina, her pen pal Alicia, and two other girls, and Papa would stay with the two boys in another room. It was the perfect arrangement.

The two boys hadn't said a word to one another, so Mimi stepped in to break the ice. "Grant, why don't you tell Mike about all the spy stuff you brought along on the trip?"

"I have some really neat spy stuff," Grant said. "You just won't believe it when you see it!"

Mike smiled. "Really? Me, too!"

"Cool!" Grant knew they'd be great friends. "Come on, let's ask Papa if we can get something to drink before we go upstairs," he said. He looked imploringly at his grandpa, and folded his hands as if in prayer. "Can we paleeeeaaasse get something to drink, Papa? It's really warm in here."

Papa noticed that the boys' faces were flushed. Plus, he was thirsty himself. "Let's go see what we can rustle up for you two," he said.

Grant and Mike stood by the snack bar while Papa ordered drinks for everyone. With his elbows propped up against the rail, Grant watched Mrs. Hudson's class settling into their small groups in the lobby.

Suddenly, Grant had the strangest feeling that he was being watched. Everything looks normal, he thought, as he scanned the crowd. He caught a movement out of the corner of his eye and turned toward the stairs. A tall, husky man stood there, wearing dark glasses and a neatly tailored black suit. He pointed to someone in the crowd. Grant scanned the room and noticed a bearded man in a similar suit nod his head. Wow, Grant thought. They looked like FBI agents on TV! But why would FBI agents be hanging around a hotel lobby filled with kids?

Grant turned to Mike. "There's a man over there, but don't look," he said, glancing again to where the tall, husky man in the dark glasses stood watching all the commotion. Suddenly, Grant's eyes got wide, and his mouth dropped open.

"What? What is it?" Mike whispered.

"He's talking right into his wrist watch!" Grant motioned with his chin.

Mike started to look over at the man when Grant stopped him.

"No, don't look at him. He'll know we're on to him," Grant whispered.

"On to what?" Mike asked, confused.

"Don't you see?" Grant replied. "They're watching something—or someone. If we interfere, we won't be able to snoop around and find out what it is."

Mike gave Grant a puzzled look. "Ohhhhh, I see...NOT!"

Grant patted his new friend on the back. "Leave it all to me, my friend. I'm a professional snooper," Grant remarked, raising his eyebrows and nodding his head.

He saw Papa approaching, so he put his finger to his lips so Mike wouldn't ask any more questions. Grant rubbed his hands together in excitement. "I think we've come to the right place for some good old-fashioned spy work!"

4 MINI MELTDOWN

"Isn't this just *way* too cool?" Christina asked, excited.

Mimi looked like she might burst into tears. "Oh, my," she sighed, putting her hand to her heart. "What have I gotten myself into?" Mimi had come to Washington, D.C. to do research on her next mystery book. Instead, she was babysitting a bunch of overexcited, overstimulated fourth graders!

Papa returned with a cool glass of iced tea for Mimi and cups of lemonade for the girls. While Mimi sipped her drink, Papa surveyed the room. The chaperones were still trying to round up the children, who scurried like ants around the lobby. He tipped his Stetson cowboy hat back, and looked up at the top of the winding staircase, unable to believe his eyes. It looked like some of the boys were deciding whether or not it was a good idea to slide down the banister.

He pretended to yawn, and stretched. "Suddenly, I'm a little tired," he remarked. "I think Grant, Mike and I are going to head on up to our suite now." He patted Mimi's hand. "You have fun with the girls, and I'll see you later."

"Thanks a lot," Mimi murmured under her breath.

An hour later, Mimi quietly entered Papa's suite. Her favorite red suit that had been crisp and clean just hours before was stained with remnants of cola and chip dip that one of the boys had tossed at a group of girls. It had missed the girls, but landed with a PLOP on a sculpture of Abraham Lincoln. Mimi was busy getting the mess out of Lincoln's beard when she heard,

Behind her, one of the boys had shaken a can of cola before opening it, and it had sprayed up Mimi's back.

She flopped down on the rose-colored sofa. Her beautiful red, wide-brimmed hat now hung limply over her forehead. It looked as tired as she felt.

Papa came out of the bedroom just as Mimi collapsed on the sofa. He sat down beside her and patted her hand. "That bad, huh?"

Mimi looked at him through glazed eyes. "Those...those...children!" she shouted, wagging her finger at the door. "I'm not going back out there, I tell you!"

"Now, now, Mimi, it can't be as bad as that," Papa said, chuckling.

One of her eyebrows shot up. "That's easy for you to say," she snapped. "I've just spent my evening helping Mrs. Hudson round up some giggling girls who had decided to take a tour of the hotel on their own." Mimi sighed. "I only came in here to catch my breath and see if you need anything before I hop into bed and hide under the covers until I wake up from this nightmare I'm having!"

Suddenly, Mimi heard urgent knocking on the door. "Mimi!" Christina yelled. "Come quick!"

5 I Spy A Spider!

"What now?" Mimi exclaimed. She sighed, hauling herself off the sofa. The knocking became more insistent. "Mimi, hurry and let us in!"

Papa threw open the door and four crying girls spilled into the room.

"My goodness, what's happened now?" Mimi asked.

"There's a HUGE spider in our bathroom!" Christina cried. The girls huddled around her.

"Way cool!" shouted Grant.

"I'll take care of it," Papa said, patting Christina's arm.

Mike came out of the boys' bedroom to find out what was happening. "What's going on?" he asked.

Grant's smile widened. "My big sister here," he pointed with his thumb, "is actually crying over an itsy bitsy spider! What a hoot!"

"I am not crying," she shot back, swiping at her eyes. "It was a really big spider, Papa!" She glared at her brother. "If you think the spider is so cool, why don't you switch rooms with us?"

"Deal!" cried Grant.

"Never mind, Grant," Papa said, casting a withering glance at his grandson. "I'll take care of the spider issue, and you guys get ready to hit the sack," he added. "I'm sure the spider needs to be rescued after all that screaming. Come on, Christina, show me where it is." He and Christina slipped out the door while Mimi calmed the frightened girls.

Grant bolted out the door behind Papa and Christina. He thought he'd toss one more dig at his sister. He was just about to shout a smart remark through her door when he saw the tall man in the dark glasses trying to open one of the doors down the hall.

Grant dashed behind a potted plant in the hallway. "Why doesn't he just use that card thing to open the door?" he whispered. "Unless...it's not his room!" Grant stuck his head out slightly so he could watch. Too late! He gasped as Mr. Dark Shades looked his way. He smiled and winked at Grant as he opened the door and slipped inside.

Now I know they're up to something, Grant thought. He tiptoed back to his suite, shut the door, and LOCKED IT!

6 BLUE LIGHT SPECIAL

"I declare the bathroom spider-free!" Papa exclaimed as he came back into his suite.

"Too late," Mimi said, shaking her head. "The other two girls went to stay with another chaperone. Mrs. Hudson said it would be okay, considering. So now that we've gained the title of 'The Spider People,' it looks like it will just be Christina, Ali and I bunking together for the rest of the trip."

With the spider issue behind them, Christina and Ali finally unpacked their suitcases. As Ali rummaged through her backpack, Christina sat down on the bed next to her. "I feel a little silly for losing it over that spider," Christina said with a shudder. "But they really creep me out!"

"Hmmm," Ali murmured as she continued to stack things on the bed.

Christina handed her friend a tube of toothpaste that had rolled across the bed. "Come to think of it, you didn't seem nearly as scared as I was when that spider jumped out of the sink. How come?"

Ali shrugged. "I'm sort of used to the unexpected. You see, my dad is an..."

"Lights out, ladies!" Mimi called from the other room.

"Awwwww, Mimi, we're still unpacking and we haven't even had time to have a good pillow fight yet," Christina said.

Mimi appeared in the doorway with her toothbrush in her hand. "We have an early day tomorrow, so finish unpacking quickly. You'll have to save the pillow fight for another day."

She let out a loud sigh. "I'm going to bed now. I think I've had just about all the fun I can stand for one day. Goodnight, girls." Mimi closed the door behind her.

"She's gone," Christina whispered.

Ali looked puzzled. "Okay, so why are you whispering? She can't hear us talking."

Christina turned abruptly. "Wanna bet? My grandmother can hear through walls!" She giggled. "When we were little, she used to tell us she has eyes in the back of her head. Grant used to look for them while she slept."

As Ali unpacked clothes from her suitcase, she glanced at Christina. "So did he ever find them?"

Christina arranged her two dolls, Savannah and Juliet, on the bed where she nestled them among the pillows. They traveled with her everywhere she went. Satisfied that they were comfortable, she turned to her friend. "No, but he still looks for them sometimes when she catches him doing something," she said with a laugh.

Christina was enjoying herself. It was so cool to have a girl her own age around. They could talk way into the night about girl stuff without Grant pestering her like he did when she had sleepovers at home.

Grant was also thrilled to be with his new friend. The boys both shook out their backpacks on the bed in their room, ready to compare spy stuff. As Mike gave his backpack one last shake to make sure it was empty, a fat silver pen plopped off the bed and rolled on the floor near Grant.

Grant scooped it up. "Wow! What a neat pen!" he exclaimed, handing it to Mike.

Mike grinned and twisted the cap. An eerie blue light came on. "Actually it's an electronic tracking pen," he said.

Grant's eyes got wide. "That's the coolest thing I've ever seen!" he exclaimed.

Mike smiled. "Yeah? Well, watch this," he said, wiggling his eyebrows. He put his mouth up to the cap of the pen. "Mike to Ali, Mike to Ali, come in."

Back in Christina's room, a faint blue light flashed on and off in Ali's backpack.

"What in the world is that, your parents checking in with you on your cell phone?" Christina asked.

Ali frowned. "No, worse. It's my brother." She reached inside her backpack and pulled out a glowing pen. Christina thought she heard something. "Is that static coming from your pen?" she asked.

Ali clicked a button at the top, and held the pen close to her mouth. "Ali to Mike." She tapped her foot as she waited for a response. "Ali to Mike," she repeated. "This better be important, Mike. You know we're not supposed to use these unless it's urgent."

OOOWEEEOOO!!

The screeching noise coming from the pen made Chrisina wince. Could this really be possible, she thought. A communicating device hidden inside an ink pen?

A familiar voice spoke through Ali's pen.

"Hi ya, sis!" Mike shouted.

Ali clicked the pen. "I've got your 'hi ya, sis'!" she said sternly. "You know Dad only wants us to use these in case of an emergency. Over."

SSHHHFFH!!

"I know, I know, but I wanted to show Grant how it works," Mike replied. "Over."

Ali turned to say something to Christina about brothers being a big pain, but the question died on her lips when she saw the look on Christina's face. Her mouth had dropped open when she heard Mike's voice come from inside the pen.

"What?" Ali asked innocently.

Christina was stunned. "Are you kidding me? That pen is only about the neatest thing I've ever seen in my life, that's all!"

"This old thing?" Ali twirled the pen around, acting as if having a radio pen was an everyday occurrence.

"You're making this up, right?" Christina shook the pen a few times. "It's a joke, right?"

Ali's eyes sparkled as she smiled. "Oh, there's more! The pen is also a recorder. It writes, it has a mini microphone, and a speaker to record and play back."

Christina put her hands on her hips. "Okay, what's the deal? No ordinary pen can do all that."

Ali decided it was time to confess her secret to Christina. "No, really, it's for real. You see, my dad is an..."

"Listen, do you hear that?" Christina asked.

"Hear what?" Ali replied.

"Like someone scratching on our door," Christina said. She knew that Mimi was already asleep in the other room, so she tiptoed out of her bedroom and peered cautiously through the peephole. She could see Grant and Mike through the magnified glass. Grant made a face at her by pulling his mouth wide with his fingers.

"Brothers," Christina mumbled, as she swung the door open.

7 LET THE MYSTERY SOLVING BEGIN!

Christina pulled her brother inside her room. "Shhhhh! Don't wake Mimi," she whispered. "She was really tired when she went to bed. What are you two doing here, anyway? Where's Papa?"

"He's asleep, too," Grant replied.

"Well, come into our room and don't make a sound." The kids tiptoed past Mimi's closed door as Christina shut the door to the hallway.

Grant told the girls about the man in the dark glasses. "First, he was down in the lobby, checking everything out, and then he broke into someone else's room. Or, at least I think he was breaking in. Something's going on around here—I just know it," Grant whispered.

Ali's eyes darted to her brother's eyes, warning him to keep silent. "Ah, um, Grant, maybe you just *think* something's going on," she stammered.

"Yeah? Well, what about this?" He pressed a crumpled piece of paper into her hand. "When we decided to come over here, I saw this piece of paper lying in the hallway near the room the man went into."

When Ali opened the paper she read,

"I wonder what that means," Grant said.

Ali shrugged her shoulders. "Maybe it doesn't mean anything, Grant."

Grant narrowed his eyes at her. "Listen, Ali, it just so happens that my sister and I are professional mystery solvers, and I tell you this is the beginning of a new mystery!" Grant whispered loudly.

"Calm down, little brother," Christina warned. She looked at the others. "So, do we solve this mystery together?" she asked, putting her hand out, palm down.

"I'm in." Grant plopped his hand on top of Christina's.

"Me, too," Mike said. Without hesitation, he added his hand to Grant's.

"That just leaves you, Ali," Christina whispered. "What do you say?"

Ali hesitated for a moment, then smiled. "I say, let the mystery solving begin!" She laid her hand over the others.

The group lowered their hands together, then raised them up, breaking their hands free. Christina ushered the two boys toward the door. "Okay, now go back to your room before Papa comes over here looking for you!"

The boys raced back to their room so fast that neither saw the man in the dark glasses on his hands and knees in the hallway, searching the floor for something.

8 COLONIAL CONSTITUTION

"Time to wake up!" cried Mimi with a sunny smile. Amid moans and groans, the girls got ready for the day within a half hour.

Mimi tapped on Papa's door. "We're ready, Mimi!" Grant shouted, bursting out the door. "We are soooooooo hungry!"

Mrs. Hudson saw Mimi enter the dining room and rushed to meet her. "Good morning," she said. "I hope you slept well."

"Like a rock," Mimi said, smiling.

"Oh, good," Mrs. Hudson remarked. "Well, what did you think of our George Washington?"

Mimi laughed. "He was wonderful! And he was a good sport about all the questions."

Mrs. Hudson nervously wrung her hands. "Well, that's what I wanted to talk to you about. The bus ride to the National Archives will take about 40 minutes. I know it's a lot to ask, but would you mind talking more about the U.S. Constitution with George Washington? Sort of bounce information back and forth to each other?"

Papa saw Mimi's eyes light up. "Sure, I'll help out," she replied.

After everyone was settled on the bus, Mimi and George Washington started up the conversation about the U.S. Constitution again.

Jaycie asked the first question. "So why did they decide to write the U.S. Constitution?"

George Washington bowed to Mimi. "Would you like to help me answer the question, fine lady?"

"Certainly, fine sir," Mimi chimed in. She turned to the children. "When the British and American Revolution ended, and America's independence was won, the former colonists had created a union of states for the first time. It seemed simple that the individual states could be both independent and united as a nation, but it wasn't."

"Aye," General Washington said. "We needed a stronger central government. So we held a convention at Independence Hall in Pennsylvania, in the same room where the Declaration of Independence was signed."

He scratched his head. "I remember we argued for months over details of the Constitution. In any event, I consider Independence Hall to be the real birthplace of the United States. Within its walls, the Declaration of Independence was adopted, and the U.S. Constitution was debated, drafted and signed."

Mrs. Hudson joined the conversation. "The U.S. Constitution was signed on September 17, 1787," she explained, "and contained exciting new ideas about government by the people and the division of power between states and the national government. The constitution was then rounded out with a Bill of Rights."

"What are they?" Katelynn asked.

Mrs. Hudson explained that the Bill of Rights were the first 10 amendments to the U.S. Constitution.

"We'll learn more about them on Constitution Day," she added, "but briefly, these amendments limit the powers of the federal government and protect the rights of all United States citizens. They guarantee basic freedoms like freedom of speech, press, and religion, and basic rights like the right to gather together and to appeal to the government if we want something changed. The Bill of Rights defines our character as a nation to this very day," she added.

As the miles rolled by on the way to the National Archives, Mimi and George Washington told the kids more interesting facts about that exciting time in America's history.

"To guide this new nation under the new Constitution," Mimi explained, "we elected our first president, General George Washington." She swept her arm toward the white-haired gentleman. "He stood on the balcony of Federal Hall on Wall Street, in New York, in 1789, and took his oath of office as the first president of the United States."

"Whoooo Hoooo!"

The kids whistled and cheered.

"Aye, I remember it well," President Washington said. "At first they didn't know how the people should address me." He chuckled. "Someone even suggested that the new president be called His Royal Highness, the President."

The kids giggled.

"Finally, they decided my title would be President George Washington." He smiled at Mimi. "It has a nice ring to it, don't you think?"

Mimi smiled back. "Yes, it does," she replied. "And children, during the first presidential election held, George Washington received a vote from every elector. He remains the only president in American history to be elected by the unanimous voice of the people."

Everyone on the bus applauded.

"Mimi and President George Washington get an A+ in history!" Mrs. Hudson shouted.

And with that, the bus pulled up in front of the National Archives building.

9 AWESOME ARCHIVES

The minute the bus stopped outside the National Archives building, the kids stood like tigers ready to pounce. Mrs. Hudson was on her feet in an instant. "Hold it right there!" she ordered. "Everyone sit down. I'd like to say a few things about our visit to the National Archives before we go in."

The children groaned and slumped back into their seats.

"First, please do not shout or run through the building," Mrs. Hudson said. "If you do, you will be removed and have to wait on the bus for the rest of us. Is that clear?"

A sea of heads nodded vigorously.

Mrs. Hudson clasped her hands. "You are going to see some wonderful things here that you will remember for the rest of your lives," she observed. "I know you may be a little disappointed, but the Declaration of Independence is barely readable," she said. "After the formation of the new government under the Constitution, the one-page Declaration of Independence was hung on the walls of various government buildings in Washington, D.C. It was exposed to damaging sunlight that caused it to fade."

When she saw the disappointed look on their faces, she decided to cheer them up. "I'm happy to announce," she said in a hopeful tone, "that the U.S. Constitution is in excellent physical condition after more than 200 years, so you'll be able to read it clearly."

The children shuffled quietly into the rotunda of the National Archives building, awed by the majesty and size of the magnificent room. They tilted their heads to gaze at its high, domed ceiling. Massive painted murals depicting the presentation of the Declaration of Independence and the Constitution decorated the walls.

The National Archives—home to history!

The dim lighting contrasted eerily with the brightness outside, and Grant had to blink several times to adjust his eyes. Just inside, a giant of a man stood guard over the building. One look at him told Grant that he meant business. Grant offered him a nervous wave of his hand, then hurried ahead to keep up with Mimi. Papa was setting up a tour of the city for later, and would be along shortly.

The children stood quietly in front of the glass cases protecting the precious documents. They understood they were in the presence of greatness.

"Look, the Declaration of Independence is just as Mrs. Hudson said," Christina whispered. The ink had almost faded away. She ran her hand over the glass. "Someday, there won't be anything left to read." It made Christina sad to think of that as she moved on. Suddenly, she came to an abrupt halt. Ali bumped into her, and in turn, Mike bumped into both of them.

There it was...the United States Constitution.

Christina stared in amazement at the black handwriting on the crinkled parchment. "I wonder who wrote that," she said softly. "It's such beautiful handwriting." Ali nodded in silent agreement. "And it is really clear for being 200 years old! Now I really want to see the Bill of Rights," she added, grabbing Ali's arm to pull her along.

Mimi and Grant were slowly shuffling down the line of documents. Grant was surprised that he was able to walk right up to these pieces of history without one person telling him not to touch anything! Grant thought that was really cool, and looked back to tell his grandmother.

Mimi was standing over a particular glass case, her face glowing. Grant leaned in to see what she was staring at and saw the scripted lettering, "We the People of the United States." Grant reached out and touched Mimi's arm. "Are you ok?"

"It's the U.S. Constitution," Mimi murmured. She ran her hand lovingly over the glass. "Ever since I was a young girl, I've been fascinated with this old document," she sighed.

Uh, oh. Grant knew he was in for information overload, but the old document was sort of neat with its crinkly edges and fancy writing.

That's where Papa found them, staring down at the glass.   Mimi was pointing out the different amendments, and reading them slowly, one by one. Grant's face lit up with relief when he spotted his grandfather. Papa chuckled, and put his arm around Mimi as she continued reading.

Grant tugged on her jacket. "I gotta go to the bathroom," he said, shuffling his feet.

"That's nice, dear," Mimi said, hardly paying attention.

Papa motioned with his head. "Go ahead and go, but don't take all day." As Grant started to walk away, Papa turned his head. "And don't wander off anywhere," Papa whispered, giving Grant a stern look.

Grant saluted his grandfather. "Yes, sir! I will hurry, sir!"

Papa chuckled at Grant's antics, and turned back to Mimi, still reading. "I'm sure we'll be standing right here in the same spot when you get back," he remarked.

10 COUNTERFEIT CONSTITUTION?

Grant rode his Heelys through an arched hallway, but couldn't find the restroom. He turned right, into another corridor, pulled in his wheels and hopped down some stairs to the next level. He found himself in the basement. Hmmm, he thought. No restroom here, either.

He scooted further along the marble floor on his Heelys. It was a silent place, and he knew he was making entirely too much noise. He decided to tiptoe so he could explore in silence. He tried the door handle of each room he passed, but they were locked. As he reached the end of the hallway, he saw a sign on one of the doors that read, "Preservation Room."

Grant remembered seeing the Preservation Room on a pamphlet all the kids were given when they arrived. He pulled it out of his back pocket. This is where they clean and maintain all the documents when they aren't on display or in the vault, he thought. "I think I'll just take a peek and see what's in here," he whispered.

Grant could easily see inside since the room was made of glass walls. He pressed his nose against the glass. "It looks like an operating room," he said to himself. Bottles of chemicals lined the shelves, and a work table sat in the middle of the room.

Clump! Clump! Clump!

Footsteps! Grant turned and saw the shadow of someone in the other corridor coming toward the hallway where he was standing. "Uh, oh, it's probably a security guard making his rounds," he whispered.

Grant frantically looked for a place to hide. He realized there was nothing between him and the oncoming footsteps but the Preservation Room. He knew he'd have a lot of explaining to do if he got caught, and Papa would be mad.

Grant turned the handle on the door to the Preservation Room. It opened! He dove into an open cabinet under the work table.

Grant held his breath as the footsteps drew near. Had he closed the door behind him? Probably not. He gritted his teeth. Now he'd be caught, and Papa would probably ground him for the rest of his life. The footsteps stopped. He didn't dare breathe.

FSHHHFFT!

The static of the security guard's radio startled Grant. Apparently, it had startled the security guard as well, because Grant heard him gasp.

FSHHHFFT!

"This is Joe. Over," the man said in a gruff voice.

More static emerged from the radio so he repeated, "This is Joe, do you copy?" There was a rustling sound as if the guard was fumbling with something. "These newfangled things," he mumbled. He stepped into the room and whacked the radio on the table right above Grant's head. There was more static as the radio crackled to life. "Stan, is that you?"

A voice finally answered. "Yeah, Joe, it's Stan. Are you somewhere you can talk? Over."

FSHHHFFT!

"Yeah, I'm down here in the Preservation Room. Over," Joe said.

After that, Grant could only hear snatches of their conversation, because Joe kept changing directions, making the signal weak. Grant opened the cupboard door slightly to hear better and nearly bumped his head into the security guard's blue trousers in front of him! He caught a few words Stan was saying...Counterfeit...

FSHHHFFT!

U.S. Constitution...

FSHHHFFT!

...Right away...

The radio crackled again, and Grant heard Stan's muffled voice but couldn't understand what he said. Joe raced out the door and yelled, "I'm on my way!"

Grant waited in the safety of his cubbyhole for a few minutes to make sure it was safe to come out. Finally, he crawled out of the cabinet, and ran out of the Preservation Room. He flattened himself against the wall and peeked around the corner to see if the security guard was still hanging around. "Whew! That was close," he said, wiping his brow with the sleeve of his jacket.

Grant's heart was pounding. Oh, my gosh! he thought. The U.S. Constitution is a counterfeit? He knew he had to get some help.

He noticed a **surveillance** camera on the wall above his head. He was sure someone would come if he could get their attention. He jumped up and down, waving his arms in front of the camera to draw the attention of the security guards.

Grant did not appear on the monitors in the security camera control room. Someone had disabled the camera in the corridor!

11 SAVOR THE FLAVOR!

"You are in BIG trouble, little brother," Christina said when Grant reappeared in the main room of the Archives.

"But..." Grant began to whine.

Before he could finish, Christina put her hand up. "Papa sent me to find you. He said you needed to meet them in the cafeteria for lunch."

"Food?" Grant could hear his tummy rumble at the thought. "What great punishment!"

"I wouldn't be so sure, hot shot," Christina advised. "Papa wasn't very happy that you took off like that. If I were you, I'd say a lot of 'I'm sorries,' and hope for the best," she said.

As the brother and sister entered the cafeteria, Papa's stern look met Grant's all the way across the room. Papa's eyes gave away nothing, but hinted of more to come later. Grant gulped. He didn't like it when Papa looked at him that way. Thank goodness it wasn't too often.

The room was buzzing with the chatter of Mrs. Hudson's excited class lining up for lunch. "Hi, Grant and Christina!" Megan called cheerily. Christina waved back.

The kids joined their grandparents at the table. "And, just where have you been, young man?" Papa asked, taking a big bite of his vegetable pizza.

Grant's mouth began to water. "I, uh, got lost? Yes, that's it, I got lost," Grant said, stumbling over his words as he watched the cheese stretch invitingly from Papa's mouth to the pizza slice.

Papa's raised eyebrow told Grant he didn't believe his explanation for one minute. "You were told to stay close," he said. "You told me you needed to use the restroom. That doesn't mean wandering off for more than half an hour. We even had the guards looking for you!" he bellowed. The people at the next table looked up at his loud voice.

"But Papa," Grant began, "there were two guards talking on a radio and they said..."

"Ah, here's our other pizza," Mimi interrupted, as the waitress set a large pepperoni and double cheese pie on the table. The aroma made Grant's mouth water and everything else about the man on the radio was forgotten for the moment.

Grant heaped a steaming slice on his plate, hesitated briefly, then added another. His brain immediately went into eating mode. "Mmmmmm," he said, taking a large bite. A long string of cheese dangled from the slice of pizza to his mouth. He slurped at the cheese until the pizza reached his mouth.

Christina glared across the table at her brother. "Oh, for heavens sake!" she groaned. "Can't you eat like a normal person?"

"What?" Grant asked. "Eating a cheesy, pepperoni pizza is an event," he said as he waved his slice of pizza under her nose. "I need to savor the flavor!"

Just as Christina opened her mouth to comment, a security guard entered the cafeteria. He was talking into his radio. As he walked past the family, he said, "This is Joe. Over."

Grant nearly choked on his pizza and started coughing. Christina jumped up as Papa patted him on the back. The guard gave them a quick glance as he passed by. Grant stopped coughing long enough to gulp down some soda.

Relieved that her brother was all right, Christina pointed and said, "See? You crammed so much food in your mouth you nearly choked to death!"

Grant looked at her with watering eyes. "Did not!"

"Did too!" Christina returned.

"Did not!"

Papa had had enough. "Okay, you two, enough already! Grant, sit down and finish eating your pizza, but slowly this time." He gave each of them a stern look. "And I don't want to hear a peep out of either of you until you are finished eating, understand?"

Both kids nodded vigorously. They knew when not to push an issue with Papa.

As the family finished their meal, Ali and Mike approached with a tall man in a tailored, expensive suit. "Hi, everyone!" Ali said cheerfully. She turned to the man. "This is Mimi, the famous mystery writer, and Papa. And this is Christina, who I'm staying with, and her brother, Grant, who Mike is staying with." She took hold of the man's hand. "And this is our father, Ag...um, William Hansen."

Papa stood and shook hands with Mr. Hansen, while Mimi daintily blotted her lips with her linen napkin as she looked up to greet him.

Mr. Hansen gave a slight bow, and smiled broadly at Mimi. "Madam, I must say that the children have spoken of nothing else but you since meeting your family." He took her hand in his and gently patted it. "I'm a big fan of yours as well," he said with a wink.

Mimi blushed at the compliment. "Please join us, Mr. Hansen." She motioned with her hand for him to sit at the table.

As he sat down, the security guard that Grant recognized as Joe passed by and nodded at Mr. Hansen in acknowledgement. He returned the nod.

As Joe walked away, Grant tugged at Papa's coat. "That's the guy I was trying to tell you about!"

"What?" In the noisy restaurant, Papa had to lean down to hear Grant better. "What did you say, Grant?"

"I said that was the guy I was trying to tell you about," Grant repeated. He turned to point to the security guard, but he had disappeared.

Grant didn't notice that Joe had doubled back and called someone on his radio. "I've got the Constitution," he said.

12 DIAGRAM DIVERSION

The kids waited at the table while Mimi and Papa paid the bill. Christina thought it would be the perfect time to hear all the details from her brother about the security guard situation earlier. She checked to make sure no one was looking. "Okay, spill," Christina urged.

Grant looked both ways once again. The kids huddled in close. "Well, there was this guard named Joe," he began.

When Grant finished his story, the others just stared at him. No one seemed willing to break the silence. Suddenly, Ali burst out laughing. "You *are* talking about the United States Constitution, right? THE Constitution?" she asked. Ali sprang out of her chair and paced in front of Grant. "It can't be done,

Grant," she said, throwing her hands wide. "No one can swap it out. It's impossible!"

"I know what I heard," Grant said through gritted teeth.

"Here, let me show you." Ali sat back down and pulled some notebook paper out of her backpack. She drew a diagram and practically thrust it into Grant's hands.

"Take a look at this," she said, pointing with her pen. "When the U.S. Constitution is on display, it is surrounded by guards and video monitors." She circled it on the paper. "All of the documents in that room are under bulletproof glass with sensors and heat monitors hidden inside." She shook her head. "No, Grant, if the U.S. Constitution was in danger or being swapped as you seem to think, this place would be crawling with police and FBI agents in a matter of minutes!" she exclaimed.

"Hey," Grant said. "How come you know so much about how those documents are protected, anyway?" He pointed his finger at her. "Maybe it's YOU who's going to swap out the Constitution!"

"Shhhh," Ali whispered. "Don't even think of saying something like that in a place like this. There are hidden surveillance cameras everywhere!"

Grant jumped to his feet. "See? There you go again! Knowing things that most normal people wouldn't know." He pointed his finger at her. " Can you explain how you know so much about the security systems in this place?" he asked.

Ali threw up her hands. "I keep trying to tell you. My dad is an..."

"Yoo-hooo! Kids!" Mimi cried out. "Ready to check out the gift shop?"

13 SECRET SWAP

The Archives gift shop was full of fascinating trinkets. Mimi looked at everything, while the girls concentrated on some of the books and handmade jewelry. Replicas of the Declaration of Independence and the U.S. Constitution were hot sellers. Some were already in frames and some were rolled up, covered in cellophane. Grant had his eye on a replica of the U.S. Constitution. He thought it would make a great gift for Mrs. Hudson.

"Can we buy it for her, Papa?" Grant asked. "Sure," said Papa. "That's a nice idea." He pulled several bills out of his money clip and gave them to Grant.

As the clerk at the counter helped Grant with his purchase, he couldn't resist asking her a question.

"Was this gift shop in the movie?" he asked. "You know, the one about the Declaration of Independence?"

She bent forward a little to let Grant in on the secret. "They built a set to look like this gift shop for the movie. Most people don't know that," she whispered.

"Your secret is safe with me," Grant whispered back. The clerk winked at him and handed him his replica of the Constitution.

Grant backed away and gave her a quick wave. He whirled around to find the others and collided with a man in a beige trench coat behind him. The man's packages shot out in every direction, and both he and Grant dropped their rolled-up Constitution replicas. One rolled under the counter and the other twirled its way up against a book stand.

"Sorry, mister," Grant said, as he bent to pick up the document by the books. He had to squirm on his belly to reach the other one under the counter. He brushed some dust off the cellophane and handed it to the man.

"Thanks, sonny," he said and hurried out of the store with his packages.

That voice! I know I've heard that voice before, Grant thought. It was Stan—the other voice on the radio this morning! Grant swung around to get a better look at the man, but he was gone.

Outside, Stan hurried to a van waiting at the curb. He quickly slid the cellophane off the Constitution and unrolled it. It wasn't the one he was carrying! He noticed his mistake at once, and pulled at his hair. "AHHHHH! All that work for nothing!" he cried.

Joe sat behind the wheel of the van. "What? What are you talking about?" he asked.

"The kid's got the real document!" Stan cried.

"What kid?" Joe asked.

"The kid in the gift shop!" Stan waved his hand. "He...never mind. I'll go back inside and get it. On second thought, how about you come with me and we'll get it done quicker."

"Let's go, Grant!" Mimi called.

"I'm coming," Grant replied, his Constitution replica tucked safely under his arm. *He didn't see the two men come back into the building, looking for him.*

14 HISTORIC HORROR

There were so many rooms still to explore in the National Archives. Blueprints, drawings, and pictures lined the walls and the halls.

"Look, it's Thomas Edison's original drawing of the electric light bulb," Christina said. She and Ali examined the rough sketch. "I wonder how he got the idea to draw something like this," she said, tilting her head this way and that.

Mimi was watching an old movie about Theodore Roosevelt, and Papa was reading about why John F. Kennedy missed 65 of 88 days in kindergarten.

Christina, Ali, Grant, and Mike wandered into another room, out of Mimi and Papa's sight. Grant was just about to say something to Christina when Stan, the man in the beige trench coat, suddenly appeared beside him. Grant moved to the right. Stan moved, too. Grant took a couple of steps back, and the man did, too.

Small prickles of fear ran down Grant's spine. Why is he doing this? Grant thought. When he glanced toward the door, he saw a bearded man waiting there, his massive build filling the doorway.

Grant felt trapped. "Come on, Christina, let's go see what's over here!" he cried. Not waiting for a reply, he grabbed his sister's hand and dragged her around the corner. Ali and Mike followed quickly.

When Grant stopped, Christina peeled his hand away from hers. "All right, Grant, what's going on?" she asked.

"There's these two men. I think they're after me!" Grant cried.

Christina was about to reply, when the man in the trenchcoat came around the corner. Christina saw him. She grabbed Grant by the hand, motioned to Ali and Mike, and quickly escaped into another room. The man followed them.

As she hustled them along, Christina was already barking orders to the rest of the kids. "Here's the deal," she whispered. "Those two guys are following

Grant for some reason," she told the others. "We'll split up, but everyone get back to Papa and Mimi QUICK! Got it?"

"GOT IT!" they all replied.

The children heard footsteps as Stan and Joe came around the corner.

"GO!" Christina shouted.

The children took off in different directions. The two men threw their arms in the air in frustration.

Christina spied Papa and Mimi looking at a display, and practically ran into them as she skidded to a stop. She grabbed Papa's hand. Grant, Mike and Ali followed suit, and gathered around them. Out of the corner of Grant's eye, he saw the two men halt abruptly at the door. They stood there for a moment, then left.

Grant heaved a sigh of relief, and nodded to his sister that the coast was clear.

"Outsmarted by a bunch of kids!" Stan roared. "That's pathetic!" *He grabbed his radio.*

15 SPY SCHOOL

Back at the hotel, the kids huddled in front of the huge fireplace in the lobby. It had grown chilly outside, so Mimi, Papa, and Mike went up to their rooms to grab their heavy jackets for the tour of the city. Mimi said she didn't want to get sick.

"I'll take your Constitution replica up to your room with me," Mimi said, watching Grant tap the scroll against his head. "That way it won't get lost."

While they waited, Christina, Ali, and Grant reviewed what had happened at the Archives. Grant felt frightened and excited at the same time. "I knew somebody was up to something!" he exclaimed.

"But what has it got to do with us?" Christina asked. "It seemed like they were after Grant for something."

Grant leaned his chin on his hands. "I don't

know what to make of it, either," he said, puzzled. "I felt like they were trying to corner me."

Christina's brows came together in a worried frown. "From now on, we all stick together, okay?"

Just as everyone nodded their heads, Mimi and Papa walked up. Mimi tossed her red striped scarf around her neck and rubbed her red gloves together. "So, are you all ready to go on the grand tour of our nation's capital?" she asked. "We're going to pack a lot in this afternoon, so let's get started!"

"Hey, Grant," Mike whispered. "This paper was on the floor near our door." Grant unfolded the handwritten note and read,

Grant gulped and handed the note to his sister. "You need to read this," he whispered.

The shiny blue double-decker bus was waiting outside. It took a few minutes for Mrs. Hudson's class to file aboard. Once everyone was seated, the tour guide began to describe the places they'd visit on their tour of Washington, D.C. The kids followed along in the pamphlet provided by the tour company.

Suddenly, Grant elbowed Mike. "Look!" he shouted, and pointed to a listing for the Spy Museum. "I bet we can find all kinds of cool stuff there!"

"Our first stop will be the International Spy Museum," the tour guide announced.

"Yesssss!"

Grant and Mike exclaimed, pumping their fists in the air.

"As a recruit in Spy School 101," the guide continued, "you will be briefed by your training officer on key sites linked to intelligence triumphs, disasters, mysteries, and hear tales of spies who've left their invisible mark on the city."

"Yes, sir! I'm in for that!" Mike cried out, giving Grant a high-five.

The boys jumped out of their seats as soon as the bus stopped. "Hey, slow down, you two," Papa said, shaking his head and chuckling. *As the boys raced into the museum, no one saw the man in the beige trench coat slip through the doorway.*

After the training officer described the equipment used by international spies, he led the group to the spy store. Grant and Mike ran from counter to counter.

"Look! Bulletproof vests!" Grant cried. "And little cameras! And tiny computers."

"My brother's really in his element now," Christina said with a laugh.

"Mine, too," Ali agreed.

"My brother would love this place," said Autumn, peeking over Ali's shoulder. "I hope he gets to go on this same field trip in two years."

A spy camera caught Grant's eye. The clerk behind the counter picked it up and said, "Smile, you're

Now that's some cool cola!

on cola camera!" She snapped a picture of Grant and Mike through the tiny lens on the cola can.

The clerk turned the cola can back and forth. "This undercover camera looks just like an ordinary cola can, but..." she said, as she pushed a tiny button on the bottom of the can, "it has a pop-up viewfinder with shutter lock, auto-focus feature, and a built-in flash."

She handed the cola camera to Grant. "Go ahead, try it. Take a *sip* and snap!"

"Coooolllll!"

Grant exclaimed as he examined the cola can camera.

The clerk smiled at her enthusiastic customers. "See how easy it is?" she asked. "Now you can keep your cover as an average cola-drinking kid, while secretly snapping a picture of your suspect."

She showed Grant and Mike their picture. It was crystal clear. "And," the sales clerk added, wiggling her eyebrows, "as an added bonus, it records, too!"

"SOLD!!" Grant cried.

Papa and Mimi were looking through some spy magazines when Grant brought his Heelys to a screeching halt right in front of them. Mimi laid her hand over her heart. "Grant, I wish you wouldn't do that! You just scared the red stripes off my scarf!"

"I'm sorry, Mimi," Grant mumbled. "Papa! Come see this neat cola camera," he pleaded. He pulled on Papa's hand and dragged him over to the counter.

Papa thought the camera was pretty cool, too. "Okay, I'll get one for each of you," he said. "You two can have a cola camera IF you promise not to cause mischief with it, and if you let me borrow it sometime," he said with a wink.

"We promise," both boys said. "Thanks, Papa!"

Papa wandered over to see what the girls were up to. Grant and Mike slipped into a back room to look at some more spy gear. They didn't see the tall man wearing a trench coat leaning against the wall.

A shadow fell over them as Grant and Mike examined a micro camera.

"G-G-Grant, do you see what I see?" Mike said, gulping.

It's him—again! Grant thought. He grabbed Mike's arm and pulled him toward the back door. Before they ran out the door, Grant yelled, "Say cheese!" and snapped a picture of the man with his cola camera.

Once outside in the alley, Grant and Mike rode their Heelys as fast as they could back to the main entrance of the museum.

Papa was just stepping out the door with Mimi and the girls. "There you are!" he exclaimed. "Where did you two disappear to?"

"Oh, we just went out the back entrance," Grant replied. *His stomach tightened as he saw the man in the trench coat standing at the curb. He shook his fist at Grant, lifted the collar of his coat, and hurried away.*

16 MONUMENT MAYHEM

"The Washington Monument was constructed in honor of George Washington," the tour bus driver explained. "The monument is among the world's tallest masonry structures, standing 555 feet in height and is made of marble, granite, and sandstone. The actual construction of the monument began in 1848, but was not completed until 1884 due to the Civil War.

"If you look up," he continued, "you'll see a difference in the shade of the marble, visible approximately 150 feet up. It clearly shows where the initial construction ended and where it resumed in 1876. Look for yourself," he added, as the bus pulled up to the monument.

The tour guide stopped Mimi and Papa as they stepped off the bus. "Oops, I almost forgot," he said, "you have exactly 45 minutes to spend here."

"Forty-five minutes!" Mimi pointed to the line waiting to get inside. "It'll take us thirty minutes just to get to the entrance!"

The guide tipped his hat. "I'm sorry, ma'am, I'm just doing my job."

Papa patted Mimi's arm. "It'll be okay, dear," he said. "I'll go ahead to the window and purchase our tickets. You and the kids can get in line. By the time I get back, you should be close to the front of the line." He shrugged. "It seems like the logical thing to do."

Mimi slid her sparkly designer sunglasses down her nose and looked at Papa over the rim. "I don't have to be logical, I'm a grandmother," she teased.

Grant stood silently in line. He kept thinking about the men following him in the National Archives and the Spy Museum. What did they want? He thought about the events of the day. The only weird thing that had happened was when he had bumped into the man with the other replica of the Constitution.

"Oh!" Grant hit his forehead with the palm of his hand. "A man wearing a beige trench coat!" he murmured. He tugged on Christina's jacket. "I was thinking..."

"There's something to get excited about," Christina said, chuckling.

There's the Washington Monument!

"Very funny." Grant blew out a breath. "Anyway, I think we need to examine that replica of the Constitution when we get back to the hotel."

"Why?" she asked.

Grant told her about his collision with the man in the beige trench coat. "I'm almost sure it was the same man from the gift shop. I think when our Constitutions hit the floor, I may have gotten his by mistake. It all happened so fast, I can't be sure, but maybe that's what he wants!"

Christina motioned with her chin. "Okay, but shhhhh, here comes Papa with the tickets."

Mimi was about to press the button on the elevator that would take them to the top of the monument when Grant cried, "Let's climb the stairs to the top! Can we Papa, can we pleeeaasseee?" He yanked insistently on Papa's jacket.

Papa winked at Mimi. "I'm game. What do you say, gang?"

"I say I'll get your head examined when we get back to the hotel," replied Mimi.

Christina, Ali, and Mike cheered.

As they went into the stairwell, none of them saw the man in the beige trench coat board the elevator.

The tour guide had told them that the Washington Monument had 893 steps, so Grant counted every one of them on the way up. "891, 892, 893!" Grant and Mike counted together as they took the last steps to the top. The girls were just a few steps back, but Papa and Mimi had fallen far behind.

The view from the top of the monument was spectacular. "Look! I can see the White House!" Christina cried. "It's soooooo beautiful!"

As Mimi reached the top, she leaned against the wall to catch her breath. "Okay, we did it," she said. "Can we please change the strategy on the way down? I vote to take the elevator."

Out of the corner of Grant's eye, he saw the man in the beige trench coat quickly marching toward them.

The other kids saw him, too.

"I think that's a great idea, Mimi," Grant said, pushing the others toward the elevator. *The man in the beige trench coat rushed to get to the elevator, but it was too late. The doors closed in his face.*

17 WHITE HOUSE WONDERS

"Next stop—the White House," the tour guide announced. "The White House is more than just the official residence of the president of the United States. It is a living museum and a testament to more than 200 years of democracy."

As they arrived at the White House gate, Christina nudged her brother. "I sure hope that creep isn't around here," she remarked with a frown. "But I don't know if we could tell anyway. Did you notice that almost every secret service man around here is wearing a beige trench coat?"

The White House tour guide explained the history of the house's architecture, furnishings, and families who had lived there as he led them through the magnificent rooms.

The girls were fascinated with the Oval Office and its blue and gold furnishings. "How do you suppose they built this round room?" Christina asked. "I want one just like it when I build my own house," she exclaimed.

Mimi's favorite was the China Room, where the delicate plate settings of the First Ladies were displayed. "Just look at those tiny coffee cups donated by First Lady Nancy Reagan," she observed. "Papa could never get his fingers inside the handle of those things!"

Papa and the boys were fascinated with the pool table in the Recreation Room. "Imagine, boys, to be able to shoot pool anytime you want," Papa sighed. "Eight ball in the side pocket!"

Soon it was time to go, and Papa rounded everyone up for the ride back to the hotel. Mimi decided she wanted to do some research for her book at the Library of Congress, so she had asked the bus driver to drop her off there. She'd meet them back at the hotel later. "Or I can stay here with you guys, if you don't want me to go," she said sweetly.

Everyone else missed Papa's "humph." He'd lived with Mimi too long to waste his breath.

The White House—where the president lives and works.

Instead, he grunted, and pulled his Stetson low over his eyes.

No one saw the man in the beige trench coat hunched down in the back seat of the tour bus.

18 You Have Bugs

"My feet hurt," Christina said, as the kids wearily trudged up to their rooms.

"I'm up for a little nap before dinner," Papa said, yawning. "That means no visitors unless absolutely necessary!"

Christina plopped into a chair in the girls' room. "I wonder if we'll have 45 minutes to eat before we have to leave again!"

KNOCK! KNOCK! KNOCK!

Christina groaned at the insistent knocking at the door.

"IT'S GONE!" Grant exclaimed, barging through the door as soon as Ali cracked it open.

"What's gone?" Christina asked, puzzled.

"The replica of the Constitution I bought today!" Grant stopped short. "Hey, maybe it's THE REAL CONSTITUTION after all!"

Ali sighed. "I thought I explained all that this morning," she said, exasperated "It is impossible to swap out the..."

RRRIIINNNGGG!

The shrill ring of the telephone on the desk startled them all.

Christina grabbed the phone. "It's Mimi," she said. "She says we all have to go downstairs right now for dinner."

"But what about the Constitution?" Grant demanded.

"It'll have to wait, little brother. I don't want Papa mad at us again," she warned.

As they headed for the elevator, Grant saw a piece of bright yellow paper on the floor near the room where the man with the dark glasses had been the day they arrived at the hotel. "I'm going to see what it is," he said to himself. He snatched the piece of paper and ran back to the others.

"Hurry up and read it," Christina said, rubbing her arms. This was beginning to give her the creeps.

"Do you think they're talking about us?" Christina asked.

"I don't know, but I'm not taking any chances," her brother said. "Wait, I have to go to the restroom, and I left my plastic key in my room," he said.

Christina reached into her pocket. "Take mine and hurry up."

"Thanks," said Grant. He pretended to head in the direction of their room. When the others turned the corner of the hallway, he quickly made his move. He made a quick stop at his room and rooted around his unmade bed for his cola camera.

Grant left his room and quietly shut the door. He tiptoed across the hall, opened the door to Christina's room and slid inside. He carefully set the cola camera recorder on a table, flipped the button to turn it on, and ran to join the others.

After dinner, Mimi and Papa had to attend a chaperone meeting in the hotel. The tour company was going to discuss the National Cherry Blossom Parade and Festival.

The kids returned to Christina's room.

As they entered the dark room, they could see a red light flashing. "What's that light flashing on the dresser?" Christina asked, anxious.

"Is it the message light for the phone?" Ali asked.

"No." Grant's brows drew together. "Bugs."

"You have bugs?" Ali asked, making a face.

"No, actually, you have bugs." Grant replied.

"He means surveillance bugs, don't you, brother of mine?" Christina said with narrowed eyes.

Grant didn't like the way she was looking at him. He was ready for the storm and she didn't disappoint him.

Christina put her hands on her hips. "That's invasion of privacy, and you know it!" She impatiently tapped her foot. "Tell me why you planted bugs in this room and I might change my mind about telling on you," Christina demanded.

Grant picked up the cola can camera from the dresser. "Actually, it was only one bug," he said. Christina's angry expression did not change. "How else was I supposed to know whether or not Ali was involved in the disappearance of the Constitution?" Grant asked.

Christina threw her hands in the air. "For goodness sake, Grant, Ali is not a spy, nor does she know anyone who is. Sometimes I don't know what goes on in that noggin of yours!" she shouted, tapping his head with her finger.

"Ouch! Okay, okay, so I went a little overboard," Grant said. The tiny light was still flashing on his cola can. "But since we were gone, and now the light is flashing, it means we got something," he added.

Grant flipped the recorder switch. Voices! Voices attached to real men who had been in their room! There were rustling sounds—were they looking through their belongings? Then a voice over a radio said, "I want an update on those kids."

"Copy that," another voice replied.

"It's not here. Let's go before they return."

Christina was baffled and a bit frightened. "What do you think they want?"

"I think they swapped out the U.S. Constitution!" Grant blurted out. "I don't know why or how, but somehow we're linked to all of it!" He shook his head. "But my copy of the Constitution is missing, too. They must have searched my room and didn't find it so they thought it was in here!"

Christina shivered and rubbed her arms. "They were in our room!" she exclaimed. "That gives me the creeps! And here you were suspecting Ali. Now you KNOW she's not a spy and doesn't know anyone who is!"

"That's not entirely true," Ali said with a shy but guilty look.

Christina whirled around. "What? Which part?"

Ali put her hands on her hips and paced across the room. "That's what I have been trying to tell you this whole time. My dad is an..."

"Shhhhhh! I hear something." Christina padded quietly across the carpet in her socks. The door handle was slowly moving up and down. The kids looked at each other in panic and huddled together. Ali's teeth chattered. "Do you think it's the bad guys coming to get us?" she whispered.

Someone slipped a plastic key in the lock, and they heard the tumblers click. By the time the door creaked open, the kids were nearly hysterical.

It was Papa! And he was holding cups of hot chocolate!

19 Top Secret

Christina was tired. After she finished her hot chocolate, she announced, "I'm going to bed!" Ali yawned. "I'm ready to go, too, so boys, get out of our room!"

"Okay, okay," Mike said. "We know when we're not wanted!" Grant and Mike slipped out the door, giggling as they headed down the hall to the suite they shared with Papa.

"I get the bathroom first!" shouted Ali, as soon as the door shut.

"Go right ahead," Christina said. "I just hope I can stay awake until it's my turn!" She unhooked the heart necklace Mimi had given her last Christmas. As she pulled the necklace from her neck, the heart slid off the chain and rolled under the bed.

"Oh, good grief," Christina said. "Where did you go?" She laid on her belly and peered under the bed. The shiny heart had rolled to the wall. Christina grabbed it, but another shimmering object caught her eye.

She stretched her arm further under the bed. Her fingertips touched a cellophane-wrapped roll. "What is this—a roll of wrapping paper?" Christina asked. As she rolled it out, she realized she had just solved one mystery—the mystery of Grant's missing Constitution replica!

"What's that?" Ali asked, looking over Christina's shoulder.

"It's Grant's Constitution," Christina replied. "I wonder what it's doing in here!" As she held it up to show Ali, the Constitution slipped out of one end of the cellophane wrapper.

"Let's look at it," Ali suggested.

"Okay," Christina replied. "I never got a good look at it in the store." Christina carefully unrolled the document, shocked to see several papers fall out. They were marked,

TOP SECRET

Ali and Christina looked at each other in amazement. "What in the world..." Ali said.

"Hey, lights out!" called Mimi from the next room.

Christina shuffled the papers in her hands, but had no idea what they were. She just knew they must be valuable.

"I'm going to sleep on this one," Christina said, rolling the mysterious papers back up into the Constitution replica. *What could this mean?*

20 PARADE OF FEAR

It was barely dawn when Mimi woke the girls. "Let's get a move on, ladies! We have to go down to the lobby and meet the others!"

"But Mimi," Christina's muffled voice came from under the covers. "The sun isn't even up yet!"

"It will be by the time we get ready and head for the buses," Mimi replied.

"What do you think about what we found last night?" Ali whispered.

"I'm not sure yet," Christina said. "But we should have time to tell the boys about it after the Cherry Blossom Festival parade." She wasn't sure why, but she decided to tuck the Constitution replica inside her jacket and take it with her.

The lobby was filled with the sound of excited children chattering. Papa stepped out of the elevator with Grant stumbling behind him. He looked like he was still asleep, with messy blond curls poking out in all directions.

"Grant, why don't you comb your hair?" Christina suggested. "It's sticking out everywhere."

Grant licked his palm and wiped his hand over his hair. "That should do it," he mumbled. "It wasn't so bad until that guy bumped into me getting on the elevator."

"What's that sticking out of your pocket?" Christina asked.

"I don't know," Grant replied. Christina grabbed the paper and unfolded it. She read,

"Those are our room numbers!" Christina cried. She stared into Grant's blue eyes. "Let's stick close together, brother." Grant nodded.

Hiding the replica!

"Okay, let's move," Papa said. "Let's herd these kids on the bus before they wreck the hotel!"

With a thump and a bump, the bus arrived in the heart of Washington for the annual National Cherry Blossom Festival Parade. As Mimi descended the bus steps, the wind whipped through her blond curls. "I hope the weather warms up a little," she said, shivering in her down-filled jacket. "Look, it's beginning to snow!" She knew that spring snow flurries were not uncommon in Washington.

Grant couldn't quite understand this celebration. "Why would anyone get all excited about trees?" he asked. He would much rather return to the spy museum.

Mimi smiled. "The trees were a gift from Japan in an effort to **enhance** the growing friendship between the United States and Japan in the early 1900s," she explained.

"Hmmmph," said Grant, not impressed.

At the beginning of the parade route, some people had come early, even before the sun rose, to set up tents, cook breakfast, and erect scaffolds for the TV cameras.

"I smell food!" Grant said, rubbing his tummy.

"I smell coffee," Papa said, blowing into his

cupped hands to warm them. "I'll be back shortly." He sped off in the direction of the coffee tent. Minutes later, he returned, carrying a bag of warm, soft doughnuts, huge cups of steaming coffee, and plenty of hot cocoa for the kids.

"Mmm, doughnuts!" Christina exclaimed. "They always manage to get stuck in my braces, but I'm eating them anyway!"

"Come on, let's find a spot where we can freeze along with the others," Papa said, pointing to where Mimi and all the other chaperones had gathered with the children.

The crowd increased by the minute despite the cold temperatures and snow flurries. The first bands marched boldly up the street.

RAT-ᴀ-TAT, RAT-Aᴛᴀᴛ-TAT

The drums' booming bass echoed from building to building.

"Hey, why aren't they playing their instruments?" Christina asked as the first band pounded past them.

"Their instruments would probably stick to their

lips if they did," Papa said, rubbing his hands together. He smiled as he watched onlookers dance to the music to keep warm.

As floats slowly cruised by, children scrambled to grab the candy tossed by the float riders. Clowns dancing with brightly colored balloons came next, followed by a squad of more than 50 women in bright red hats.

"Look, Mimi, they're all wearing hats just like yours!" Christina exclaimed.

"Those women are members of the National Red Hat Society," Mimi explained, waving excitedly to the women. "It's a special organization for women over 50! Their mission is to gain higher visibility for women in the '50 and older' age group, and to reshape the way they are viewed by today's culture."

"Are you a member of their organization?" Christina asked.

"Who said I'm over 50?" Mimi said with a smile.

Grant was more interested in the events of the parade. He watched a group of famous cartoon and movie characters toss candy to the crowd and play with the children. They were also holding the lines to what had to be the largest balloon in the parade history—Superman! It took 20 characters to keep him from flying away.

A thought suddenly struck Grant. If someone had swapped out the U.S. Constitution, the best time to get it out of town would be during the parade, this weekend, when the police would be distracted by all the people!

Grant slid next to his sister. "We have to save it!" he whispered.

21 SUPERHERO IN THE SKY

Christina wanted to tell Grant what she had found but the time wasn't right. Besides, there was a more pressing matter at hand. "Oh, my goodness—look at that!" Christina cried.

The massive Superman balloon looked like it was out of control. It dipped lower...lower...lower...until it was directly over Grant's head! Christina yelled at him and motioned frantically. *What is she saying? I can't hear a thing over the band,* Grant thought. Christina was pointing to something in the sky. He looked up and saw...Superman's bicep muscle coming down right on top of him!

"Grant, get out of the way!" Christina shrieked. People around him scattered.

Too late! Christina's jaw dropped as Superman engulfed her brother.

Grant was pinned to the ground by an enormous foot on his chest. He wiggled and squirmed, but couldn't free himself. Suddenly, a man lifted up a flap of the flattened balloon. His face was covered by a ski mask except for his eyes and mouth. He reached for Grant. "Okay, kid, you're coming with me!" he shouted.

What came next seemed like it was happening in slow motion. As Grant watched, Superman's fist swung down, catching the man in the mask right in the face just as Grant moved out of his reach.

Thud!

The man hit the ground like a rock.

The diversion gave Grant time to wiggle out from under Superman, and roll out into the daylight. The man in the mask scrambled to his feet.

Christina and Ali stood, frozen, watching the man run after Grant.

Mrs. Hudson and her class had witnessed everything from across the street. "We've got to help Grant!" cried Justin. The class raced to follow Grant, dodging frantic parade watchers scattering across the parade route. Brody pointed to the man in the beige trench coat who was chasing Grant. "HEY! STRANGER!" he screamed.

The man caught up with Grant just short of the curb and thrust out a hand to grab him. Seeing that Mike and several of the other children were near, Grant spun around and let out a mighty

Keeeeyaaaa!

He laid a karate chop on the man's wrist while Mike stomped hard on his foot.

Owwwwwwww!

The man grabbed his wrist and hopped on one foot just as Papa, Mimi, and two policemen rounded the corner.

"I think that's the guy who's been chasing us!" Grant shouted, gripping Christina's arm.

"Wow! I've got to get my dad!" Mike shouted.

Grant was puzzled. "Your dad? What can he do?"

"You don't understand, he's an..." Mike called over his shoulder.

"WHAT IS GOING ON HERE?" Papa demanded in a booming voice.

22 You're Guilty, Mister!

Christina flew into Papa's arms, where she knew she'd be safe. She knew it was time to tell him what was happening. The events of the parade had scared her, and she knew they needed help from the adults. The policemen held tight to the struggling man in the ski mask.

"Papa," Christina said quietly, "we need to talk to you."

He looked at the four frightened faces, and shook his head. "I was afraid of that."

When Papa heard their story, he said to Mimi, "You and the kids go on into that diner behind us and keep warm. I think it's time to head to the police station with these officers and that fellow over there." He motioned with his thumb toward the man in the ski mask behind them.

"There's no need for that," Ali said. As everyone swung around to face her, her father walked up and showed Papa and Mimi his badge.

Ali spread her arms wide. "This is what I've been trying to tell you!" she exclaimed. "My dad is an FBI agent!"

Grant and Christina were stunned.

"Cool!" Grant cried, and gave Mike a high-five.

Papa stepped forward and put out his hand. Mr. Hansen shook it. "Mr. Hansen, I mean Agent Hansen, I don't know what this is all about, but if it's all right with you, I say let's talk about this over a cup of coffee." Agent Hansen nodded in agreement.

Papa opened the door to the diner, and the group piled into the warm, sunny dining room. The two policemen followed with the man in the ski mask.

Mrs. Hudson and the children followed them inside. The kids filled every nook and cranny in the diner. They were strangely quiet, sensing that something important was happening.

Agent Hansen pulled out a chair for Mimi. He motioned for Papa to sit in the other.

"I think I'll just stand here, if you don't mind," Papa said with a worried look.

Agent Hansen sighed. "I guess it's best to start at the beginning. We knew something suspicious was going on at the National Archives, but we needed hard evidence."

"Did they swap out the U.S. Constitution?" asked Grant.

Agent Hansen ruffled Grant's hair. "I'm afraid that's impossible, young man. You see, when the Constitution is not on display, it is lowered into a four-inch-thick, concrete, steel-plated vault with an electronic combination lock and biometric access denial systems."

At Grant's astounded look, Agent Hansen smiled. "Pretty cool, huh?"

Grant smiled. "Waaaaaay cool!"

Christina raised her hand to ask a question, even though she thought she knew the answer. "So, if the Constitution is safe, what were they after, and what did we have to do with it?"

"I know it had something to do with my copy of the Constitution, if only they hadn't stolen it," Grant said looking sad and disappointed.

"Your copy of the Constitution...oh, Grant, I'm so sorry," Mimi said. "I put it in Christina's room because I was going to frame it as a birthday present for you."

So that's why it was under my bed, Christina thought.

"I can't believe it! I thought it was stolen!" Grant exclaimed.

Agent Hansen continued. "We think the copy Grant has was being used for a sinister purpose."

Papa looked confused. "What are you talking about?" he asked.

"I think I can answer that," Christina said. All the adults whirled around to look at her, including Agent Hansen. She whipped the Constitution replica out of her jacket.

"Look what's rolled up in *this* Constitution," Christina explained. She pulled the replica out of its plastic sleeve and unrolled it on the table.

"Whooooooaaaa!" Grant cried. The papers marked,

fluttered onto the table. "They've been smuggling out important documents in Constitution replicas!" Christina cried.

"You're absolutely right, Christina, and you're guilty, mister!" Agent Hansen exclaimed, pointing to the man in the ski mask. The officers yanked off the mask and revealed the scowling face of Joe, the guard from the National Archives.

Agent Hansen folded his hands across his chest. "Our friend Joe here seems to be a bungling thief," he remarked. "He thought he was being slick, but his erratic behavior soon attracted the suspicions of the staff, and we were called."

Papa's eyebrows drew together. "What did he do that got your attention?"

"People often forget that we have surveillance cameras located throughout the Archives building," Agent Hansen explained. "He was observed taking important documents out in both his pants and his socks. He turned them over to his partner, who rolled them up in a replica of the U.S. Constitution. He stopped in the gift shop to purchase a pack of gum, when you bumped into him, Grant."

Agent Hansen bent to retrieve the documents. "Joe was observed leaving the building and then hiding papers under a trailer at a nearby construction site, presumably for later pickup by his partner, Stan," he said. "That's the day you kids saw him in the alley."

"Because of the FBI's mounting suspicions," Agent Hansen added, "officials at the Archives arranged a sting operation by numbering various documents to catch poor Joe red-handed. We got a search warrant to go through his apartment, but didn't find anything. Now that Christina has produced these documents, we know we have our man!"

Grant looked thoughtful and began to pace the room. "If their mission wasn't to swap the Constitution, then that can only mean one thing," he said.

"They were trying to create a diversion!" Christina and Grant blurted out in unison.

"Right you are!" Agent Hansen exclaimed. "Joe was never going to swap the U.S. Constitution. He just wanted the FBI to think he was, so he could cover up his attempt to steal these secret documents." Agent Hansen smiled at Mimi and Papa. "Everyone can breathe easier now. The real Constitution is right where it belongs, safely inside the National Archives."

Joe started to squirm against his handcuffs. "If it weren't for you meddling kids, I'd be out of the country right now," he cried.

"Quiet!" Agent Hansen warned. "We'll get to you in a minute."

He turned back to Mimi and Papa. "You have some very smart and brave grandchildren," he remarked. "I hope you and your family will accept my **apology** that you got involved in official government business while visiting our nation's capital."

Agent Hansen reached into his suit jacket and removed two billfolds. He handed one to Grant and the other to Christina. "Thank you both for helping the United States government crack this case and catch the thief," he said, smiling. "You are now honorary members of the FBI."

Christina and Grant opened the billfolds. There, lying on a bed of blue velvet, were copies of official FBI badges. All the kids clapped!

"Wow!" Christina said with a gasp.

"We didn't realize how many new agents we'd have today, Mrs. Hudson," Agent Hansen added. "Someone will drop off badges for your entire class before you leave town."

Mrs. Hudson and Mrs. Whatley beamed with pride. "Thank you!" Mrs. Hudson said.

Grant flipped his billfold closed. "I really like it," he remarked, "but I was kind of hoping for a spy pen."

Agent Hansen ruffled Grant's hair. "Maybe next time!" he said with a chuckle. He shook Papa's hand, and then held Mimi's hand up to his lips and kissed it. "Madam, it has indeed been a great pleasure meeting you. I can't wait to read your next book," he added.

"Humph," said Papa with a sigh. "There'll be no living with her now!"

The End

About the Author

Carole Marsh is an author and publisher who has written many works of fiction and non-fiction for young readers. She travels throughout the United States and around the world to research her books. In 1979 Carole Marsh was named Communicator of the Year for her corporate communications work with major national and international corporations.

Marsh is the founder and CEO of Gallopade International, established in 1979. Today, Gallopade International is widely recognized as a leading source of educational materials for every state and many countries. Marsh and Gallopade were recipients of the 2004 Teachers' Choice Award. Marsh has written more than 50 Carole Marsh Mysteries™. In 2007, she was named Georgia Author of the year. Years ago, her children, Michele and Michael, were the original characters in her mystery books. Today, they continue the Carole Marsh Books tradition by working at Gallopade. By adding grandchildren Grant and Christina as new mystery characters, she has continued the tradition for a third generation.

Ms. Marsh welcomes correspondence from her readers. You can e-mail her at fanclub@gallopade.com, visit carolemarshmysteries.com, or write to her in care of Gallopade International, P.O. Box 2779, Peachtree City, Georgia, 30269 USA.

Built-In Book Club
Talk About It!

1. How would you feel if your grandmother went on a field trip with your class?

2. If you went to Washington, D.C., what places would you like to visit? Why did you choose them?

3. Would you want to walk up the 893 steps to the top of the Washington Monument, or take the elevator? Which do you think would be more fun?

4. Christina and Ali had a spider in their bathroom! Have you ever been frightened by a spider or some other insect?

5. Grant and Mike convinced Papa to buy them cola spy cameras. If you had a spy camera, what would you do with it? Who would you spy on?

6. If your house had a recreation room like the White House, what kind of games would you put in there? Would the room be a normal room with four walls or would it be a fun shape?

7. Who was your favorite character in the book? Which character is most like you?

8. What was your favorite part of the book? Why was that part your favorite?

Built-In Book Club
Bring It To Life!

1. Establish your rights! Have your book club come up with your own Constitution or Bill of Rights. Let each person make up their own amendment and why they think it is important.   You could also write a bill of rights for a big brother or a big sister. Think of rights that you want to have and that you think others should have as well.

2. Pretend that you are the president of the United States. Draw a picture of the way the White House would look if you were in office. Include any interesting rooms that you would add. Would you add an indoor pool? A trampoline room? What about a room full of jell-o?

3. Use the Internet to learn more about your favorite president. Find out about his childhood. Where was he born? Did he have any brothers or sisters or was he an only child? Did he have any pets? How did he become the president?

4. Make your own spy equipment out of everyday objects. You could make a telescope out of a paper towel roll. You could make secret x-ray sunglasses or a pen that writes in invisible ink.

5. Have a parade with your book club that celebrates our nation's history and capital. Make sure you wear red, white and blue! Carry flags and sing patriotic songs like the "Star Spangled Banner." You could even dress up like Uncle Sam!

G LOSSARY

SAT **apology:** an expression of regret

SAT **conversation:** the use of words to share views, ideas or information

exuberance: overflowing with joy

significance: the meaning and value of something

unanimous: in complete agreement

counterfeit: not real; an imitation

SAT **surveillance:** close observation of a person or group

replica: a copy; a reproduction

diversion: a turning of attention to something else

erratic: unpredictable; likely to change suddenly

SAT **enhance:** increase; make better

SAT **commotion:** a noisy disturbance the thief?

CONSTITUTION TRIVIA

1. Only 12 of the 13 states were represented at the Constitutional Convention. Rhode Island was the only state not to send anyone to the convention.

2. The Constitution was written in 1787 but did not become law until June 21, 1788 after two-thirds of the states ratified it. Not all the states had ratified it by April 30, 1789 when George Washington became the first president of the United States.

3. James Madison is known as the "Father of the Constitution."

4. When writing the Constitution, the delegates made sure that what went on inside the convention was a secret. Dirt was spread on the streets to muffle the sounds outside the Pennsylvania State House. There were even armed guards to protect the secrecy of the meetings!

5. The U.S. Constitution has 4,400 words. It is the oldest and shortest written constitution of any major government in the world.

6. Benjamin Franklin was in such poor health that he needed help to sign the Constitution. Tears ran down his face. He was 81 years old.

7. When the Japanese bombed Pearl Harbor in 1941, the Constitution was moved from the National Archives to Fort Knox in Kentucky.

8. The word "democracy" does not appear once in the Constitution.

9. The United States' population was 4 million when the Constitution was signed. Today, the U.S. population is more than 300 million!

10. Gouverneur Morris of New Jersey wrote the final form of the Constitution by hand. He completed this huge task in only two days!

WOULD YOU LIKE TO BE A CHARACTER IN A CAROLE MARSH MYSTERY?

If you would like to star in a Carole Marsh Mystery, fill out the form below and write a 25-word paragraph about why you think you would make a good character! Once you're done, ask your mom or dad to send this page to:

Carole Marsh Mysteries Fan Club
Gallopade International
P.O. Box 2779
Peachtree City, GA 30269

My name is: _____

I am a: _____boy _____ girl   Age: _____

I live at: _____

City: _____ State:_____ Zip code: _____

My e-mail address: _____

My phone number is: _____

_____
_____
_____
_____
_____
_____
_____
_____
_____
_____

VISIT THE CAROLE MARSH MYSTERIES WEBSITE

www.carolemarshmysteries.com

- *Check out what's coming up next! Are we coming to your area with our next book release? Maybe you can have your book signed by the author!*

- *Join the Carole Marsh Mysteries Fan Club!*

- *Apply for the chance to be a character in an upcoming Carole Marsh Mystery!*

- *Learn how to write your own mystery!*